This book belongs to

_____

Published by Scholastic Inc., 90 Old Sherman Turnpike, Danbury, Connecticut 06816.

ISBN: 0-7172-9959-7

Printed in the U.S.A.

First Scholastic printing, July 2006

The Fastest Dodge Ball in the West

A Lesson in
Doing Good Deeds

by
Doug Peterson

Illustrated by
Tom Bancroft
and **Rob Corley**
Colored by Jon Conkling

SCHOLASTIC INC.

New York Toronto London Auckland Sydney
Mexico City New Delhi Hong Kong Buenos Aires

"Grrrrr

rrrrrrrrrrrrrrrrrrrrrr!

The burly cowpoke struggled to get ketchup out of the
squirt bottle. (Cowboys growl a lot when they're angry
and hungry.)

"Allow me," said Cowboy Larry, who worked
at the Wyatt Slurp Café. "There's a secret to
unclogging ketchup bottles. You just tap
right here and . . ."

Squirt!

"Oops," said Cowboy Larry.

"Grrrrrrrrrrrrrr!"

(Cowboys growl even more when they're hungry, angry, **and** covered in ketchup.)

Everyone at the table jumped up so fast that their chairs fell over.

"Grrrrrrrrrrrrrrrrrrrrrrrrrrrrrrrrrr!"

"Was that a laugh or a growl?" Cowboy Larry asked, backing up faster than a horse in a snake pit. "Sometimes it's hard to tell."

"Grrrrrrrrrrrrrrrrrrrrrrrrr!" The cowboys

forced Cowboy Larry into a corner.

"That's definitely a growl," said Cowboy Larry, grabbing another ketchup bottle. "But I really didn't mean to squirt you. I was just showing that if you tap it here . . ."

SPLURT!

Cowboy Larry did it again. He shot another stream of ketchup, splattering a second cowboy.

"Make that double oops," Cowboy Larry said, looking for an escape.

Now, there were three loaded ketchup bottles pointed at the trembling cucumber. They moved in closer and . . .

Whap! Whap! Whap!

Three dodge balls zipped across the room. With perfect aim, the balls knocked the ketchup containers cleanly out of the grasp of the angry cowboys.

All eyes turned toward the swinging doors of the restaurant.
Standing there was none other than the heroic Sheriff Bob the Tomato—
the **Second** Fastest Dodge Ball in the West. He had saved the day!

The cowboys took five angry hops toward
the lawman. They locked eyes. The tension
in the room was thicker than flies around a
skunk's sock drawer . . .

Suddenly Sheriff Bob said with a smile, "You know, if you want to get those ketchup stains out, first you should scrape them with a dull knife and then blot them with a wet sponge."

"Really?" one of the cowboys said. "I usually have my cattle stomp on my clothes. *Then* I blot with water. Your idea sounds better."

For the rest of the morning, Sheriff Bob and the cowboys shared tips on how to get rid of stains. He even told the cowboys that he would take their ketchup-covered shirts to the Red River Laundromat to clean them himself.

Sheriff Bob was always doing good deeds like that. He knew that doing good deeds helps make good friends. And he had just made good friends with these boys.

As Sheriff Bob used stain remover on one of the shirts, a little French buckaroo dashed into the laundromat.

"Sher-ee-ff Bob! Trouble eez coming!" he shouted, hopping up and down. "Rattlesnake Ricky has just gotten out of zee Buzzard Neck Jail. And he'z coming to get you!"

WASH and FLUFF 50¢

Sheriff Bob thought back.
He was the one who put Rattlesnake
Ricky in jail for rustling grocery carts.

Rattlesnake Ricky was probably on his way seeking his
revenge. He also happened to be **The** Fastest Dodge Ball
in the West.

"I can call you a taxi if you need to get out of town," said Cowboy Larry.

"I'm *not* gonna run from Ricky," Sheriff Bob said bravely. "I'm sheriff, and I've got a lot of good deeds to do today."

And that's exactly what Sheriff Bob did.

He helped Mayor Nezzer mow his tumbleweeds.

He helped Miss Kitty get her Cool Ranch Buffalo Chips out of the vending machine.

He even gave Cowboy Larry lessons on hurling dodge balls.

Then later that afternoon, a cloud

of dust was spotted on the horizon.

"Zee horse! Zee horse!" shouted the

little buckaroo. "Rattlesnake Ricky eez here!"

Frightened women
hurried children into
buildings. Scared cowboys
ran for cover. Only Sheriff
Bob and Cowboy Larry
stood their ground.

Rattlesnake Ricky reached the edge of town. The big pickle hopped off his wooden horse and moseyed down the street.

"Do you have my dodge balls?" Sheriff Bob whispered to Cowboy Larry.

"Sure thing, Sheriff Bob," said Cowboy Larry, as he handed the sheriff one of the dodge balls.

The sheriff stared at the ball in shock. "It's *flat*," he said.

"That's right," whispered Cowboy Larry. "I learned something important today. Never throw dodge balls at a cactus for target practice."

Cowboy Larry handed Sheriff Bob four more dodge balls. All of them were as flat as a 10-gallon hat under a water buffalo. Cowboy Larry was really starting to worry about what might happen to Sheriff Bob.

"Sheriff Bob, I've been lookin' for ya,"
snarled Rattlesnake Ricky.

Without a dodge ball, Sheriff Bob was in big trouble.

(Was this the end of Sheriff Bob? Were his days of doing good deeds over? Would Rattlesnake Ricky run Sheriff Bob out of town for good? Will these questions ever end?)

All at once, Rattlesnake Ricky broke into a big smile. He dropped his dodge ball and ran across the dusty street to greet Sheriff Bob.

"I am *SOOOOOOO* happy to see ya, pardner!" said Ricky with a laugh.

Cowboy Larry was puzzled. "Don't you want to get back at Sheriff Bob for putting you in jail?" he asked.

"Of course not!" Ricky exclaimed. "Sheriff Bob was the only person who visited me in jail! He brought me cakes and cookies, and he even read some stories to me!"

Sheriff Bob was only the Second Fastest Dodge Ball in the West. But he was definitely the Fastest *Good Deed Doer*. And this time doing good deeds had made him a good friend.

"From now on, I'm gonna do nothing but good deeds!" Ricky said. "And it's all thanks to my friend Sheriff Bob."

For his first good deed, Rattlesnake Ricky treated Sheriff Bob and Cowboy Larry to some big, juicy burgers at the Wyatt Slurp Café. It was a beautiful end to a glorious day.

"Now, if I can only get the ketchup out of this bottle for my fries," growled Rattlesnake Ricky.

Let us consider how we can stir up one another to love.
Let us help one another to do good works.
Hebrews 10:24